THE POSTMAN PAT ANNUAL
is written by Ann Burnett &
Donna Bryant

Illustrated by Joan Hickson

© Woodland Animations Ltd. 1986

Postman Pat
Annual 1987

Dear Boys and Girls,
Here is a special book just for you. There are lots of stories about my friends in Greendale and plenty of things to do. You could start with the puzzle on the next page. Have fun!
Love from,
Postman Pat
and Jess XXX

P.S. Don't forget to enter the competition at the back of this book!

Look closely at these pictures. There are ten differences. See if you can spot them.

The charity car wash

1 "Will you bring your van to the school this afternoon?" Julian asked. "To the school?" said Pat. "Whatever for?"

2 "We're having a charity car wash," said Julian. "I'll come after my round," Pat said. "It will need a wash by then."

3 It was raining hard when Pat set off. He drove through puddles. Splash! Dirty water covered the wheels.

4 Slurp! Pat drove into a muddy patch at Thompson Ground. "My van is going to be very dirty today," Pat said.

5 The big milk-tanker was just leaving Greendale Farm as Pat arrived. Splo Mud splashed over Pat's windscree

6 By the time Pat reached the school, his van was a sorry sight. "Goodness!" said Julian. "What a lot of mud."

7 "Leave it to us," said Katy and Tom. "We will soon have it clean." Julian brought soapy water and cloths.

8 Pat went into the school for a cup of tea. He looked at the drawings on the walls. "I like that giraffe," he said.

9 When Pat came out, his van was completely covered in soap suds. Katy and Tom were rubbing it clean.

10 "Now we'll hose off all the suds," Julian said. "Watch this, Dad." He turned on the hose. Whoosh!

11 In a moment, the van was sparkling clean. "It looks great," said Pat as the twins dried it off. "Thank you."

The Greendale folk have been to the charity car wash. Can you match them with their vehicles?

Tom and Katy are blowing lots of beautiful bubbles. Can you count them? 38

The chimney sweeps

1 "Oh, dear," said Granny Dryden. "I can't get my fire to burn. The smoke is coming into my living-room."

2 "Your chimney probably needs a clean," said Pat. "It must be full of soot. I'll ask Ted Glen to have a look."

3 Next day, Ted arrived with his ladder. "I'll go on the roof and drop the brush down," he said. "Watch inside, Pat."

4 Ted pushed the brush down. At first, it would not budge. Ted pushed even harder. "I can't see it!" shouted Pat.

Suddenly, Ted's brush shot down. Whoosh! A huge cloud of soot fell down the chimney. "Help!" cried Pat.

6 Ted came down to see what had happened. "Goodness!" he said. Pat wiped the soot from his glasses.

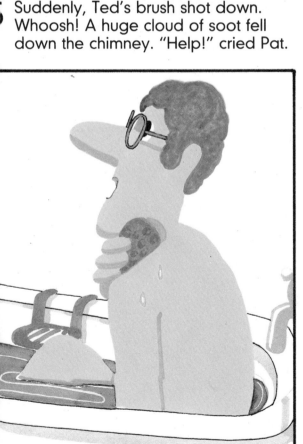

Then he washed in Granny Dryden's bath while she brushed his uniform. "Pom pom te pom," sang Pat.

8 "My fire burns beautifully now," said Granny Dryden. "There was a lot of soot up there," said Pat, laughing.

Brushes and brooms

Which brush is the same as the one Sam is holding?
What are the other brushes called? Match them into pairs.

toothbrush, nailbrush, hairbrush, scrubbing-brush, broom.

Look closely at this picture. Can you see eight things that are a little strange?

The troublesome television

Pat was tired. He had been delivering letters all day and now that he was home he just wanted to sit down and rest.

"I'll watch television for a while," he said. "My favourite programme will be on soon."

He made a cup of tea and sat down in front of the television. He switched it on and tuned it to the correct channel. Nothing happened. The screen was blank and there was no sound.

"Bother," said Pat, twiddling all the knobs. "Don't tell me it has broken down. Just when I wanted to watch it, too."

Then he saw Ted Glen passing in his Land Rover.

"Yoo hoo, Ted!" Pat called. "Can you fix the television?"

"What's it doing then?" asked Ted as he came in.

"It's not doing anything," Pat replied. "There's no sound and no picture."

"That sounds bad," said Ted, switching it on and turning the knobs. "I don't think I'll be able to do much with it."

Pat groaned. "And I want to watch a programme, too."

Ted looked at the back of the television.

"Can't see anything," he muttered as he peered into it. "I wonder what can be wrong?"

Just then Julian came in.

"Hello, Dad," said Julian. "What's up?"

"The television isn't working," Pat told him. "And Ted doesn't know what is wrong with it."

"I can tell you," said Julian, laughing. "Look!"

Pat and Ted looked.

"You've forgotten to plug it into the wall socket," giggled Julian.

"Well I never!" said Pat. "Silly me!" He put in the plug and switched it on. The television sprang into life.

"I can watch my favourite programme now," said Pat. "Thank you, Julian. How about a nice cup of tea, Ted?"

"Don't mind if I do," said Ted. "Fancy us not noticing it wasn't plugged in!"

Julian's television set

Carefully cut slits in the ends of
an empty tissue-box. Paint
knobs and switches on the box.

Draw pictures on a very long
strip of paper. Attach one end
to a pencil. Thread the picture
strip through the tissue-box and
wind it on to another pencil.

The pictures will move across
your television screen as you
wind them from one pencil to
the other.

Here is a story about Postman Pat.

Some of the pictures are muddled up. See if you can put them in order so that you can tell the story.

Send in the clowns

1 "Boo!" said a voice as a strange face peered into Pat's van. "Who is it?" Pat asked. "It must be either Katy or Tom."

2 "It's me!" shouted Katy. "I painted her face," said Tom. "She's a clown." "I like your big red nose," said Pat.

3 "Will you paint my face, Pat?" asked Tom. "That will be fun," said Pat. "I'll take off my jacket in case I ruin it."

4 Katy and Tom showed Pat their special face paints. "It washes off," said Tom. Pat put white paint over Tom's face.

5 "Make my eyes look funny," said Tom. Pat drew big crosses on them. "Now give me a red nose." Pat coloured it.

6 "Oops!" said Pat. "I've rubbed some red paint on my cheek." "Never mind," said Katy. "We'll paint your face next."

7 Pat drew a big smiling mouth on Tom. "You look like a real clown," he said. "Now it's your turn, Pat," said Katy.

8 Pat sat down and the twins set to work on him. "I haven't any more red paint," said Katy. "I'll make your nose blue."

9 Tom drew purple eyebrows and big green eyes. "I hope it does wash off," said Pat. "I have letters to deliver."

10 Mrs Pottage came in with some old clothes for them to dress up in. "Pat!" she said. "I didn't recognise you."

11 "Let's play at circuses," said Katy as they dressed up. "Isn't this fun?" said Pat. "Roll up, roll up for the circus!"

A picture to colour

Clown masks

You can make clown masks by drawing faces on paper plates. Add hair made from paper or wool. Here are some ideas.

It was a warm sunny day. Pat decided to have his lunch in a field near Greendale Farm.

"We can have a picnic," he told Jess.

Pat found a comfortable spot under a shady tree and shared his favourite sandwiches with Jess. Afterwards, Jess curled up and went to sleep.

"Ho hum," yawned Pat. "I'll have forty winks, too."

Pat had just closed his eyes when he heard a rather loud trumpeting. There in front of him was a large grey elephant.

"Oh dear," said Pat. "It's time to do the rest of my round."

Pat climbed on to the grey elephant's broad back and it set off. It swayed as it walked and Pat hung on tightly.

"Oh, er, it's a very long way down," he said to himself as the elephant plodded along. They stopped at Miss Hubbard's house. She was very angry when she saw the elephant.

"It's trampling all over my flowers," she said. "Take it away, Pat."

"I'm sorry, Miss Hubbard," said Pat. "Come on. Er, gee up!"

Next, they went to Doctor Gilbertson's. She was not pleased to see the elephant either.

"It's frightening my patients," she said. "Please don't bring it again."

The elephant seemed to be annoyed by all this fuss and it went faster and faster. Pat could not hold on. He slipped off on to the ground. The elephant's enormous feet were getting closer and closer . . .

"Help!" shouted Pat.

"Moo!" said a cow which was looking down at him.

Pat sat up. He was still in the field and Jess was asleep beside him.

"It was all a dream," said Pat to the cow. "Thank goodness for that. I'm glad I don't really do my round on an elephant!"

"If I really delivered the mail by elephant," said Pat, "I would need to give it a lot to eat!" Can you help them reach the elephant's lunch?

Pretend to be an elephant!

Make a head-band from folded newspaper.
Add big newspaper ears. You could fringe some
paper for a tail. Swing a sock from your nose
like a trunk. Plod around the room.

Sam delivers the mail

1 "Sam!" Mrs Goggins called. Sam Waldron pulled up outside the Post Office and got out of his van. "What's up?" he asked.

2 "Pat is at the dentist today," she said. "Can you deliver the mail for him?" "Of course," said Sam. "That will be easy."

3 Sam called at Ted Glen's. "Nothing today," said Ted. "I've brought your letters," said Sam. "Pat's away."

4 "Thanks," said Ted. "Can you hold this wood while I saw it in half?" Sam held on tightly while Ted sawed away at it.

5 "Letters, Doctor Gilbertson," said Sam. "Where's Pat?" she said. "I want him to take this medicine to Mrs Pottage

6 "I'll do it," Sam said. He set off for Greendale Farm. "Where's Pat?" asked the twins. "We want to play."

7 Sam played with them instead. "I must be going," he said at last. "Bye!" He drove down to Colonel Forbes place.

8 Colonel Forbes was standing at his gate. "Have you seen Pat?" he asked. "He's at the dentist today," said Sam.

9 "I want to post an airmail letter," said Colonel Forbes. "How much will it cost?" "Er, I don't know," said Sam.

10 Sam was glad when he had finished. Pat was waiting at the Post Office. "How did you get on?" he asked.

11 "It wasn't easy," said Sam. "I had to saw wood, deliver medicine and play hide-and-seek. I'm exhausted!"

"Sam starts with s," said Pat. "But I can't think of anything else." Can you? There are ten other things starting with s in this picture.

Postman Pat's Post Office

Postman Pat and Julian love playing Post Offices. They write letters and put them in old envelopes. Then they post them in a tissue-box. They use buttons and milk-bottle tops as money and take turns at serving and being a customer.

Mrs Goggins jigsaws

When it is quiet at the Post Office, Mrs Goggins likes to do a jigsaw.

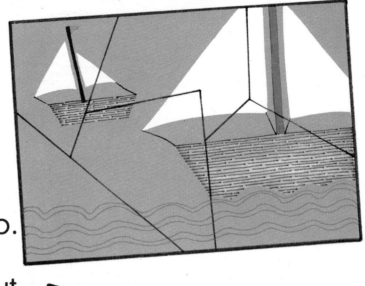

Sometimes, she makes her own. You could make some, too. Draw shapes on a postcard. Cut them out.

Jumble the pieces and then see if you can fit them together again.

Can you read this special letter?

Dear 

Today [grandma] and [eye] made a [snowman]. Please come 2 see it. We could go on the [sledge]. [girl] has baked lots of [cakes]. Love to [cat] from [woman] xxx

Mrs Goggins lost leaflet

Mrs Goggins was crocheting a shawl for Granny Dryden.

"Three trebles, miss one . . oh dear," she said. "This is a very difficult pattern to follow."

She peered closely at the instructions in the leaflet. Just then, Pat came in to pick up the mail.

"Good morning," he said, cheerily. "What are you making?"

"It's a shawl," Mrs Goggins said, holding it up. "But it's quite hard to do. The pattern is rather complicated."

"I'm afraid I can't help," said Pat. "I don't know anything about crochet." He collected the letters and set off on his round. For the next hour, Mrs Goggins was busy serving the customers who came in. But then there was a quiet spell.

"I'll try my crochet again," she said. "Now where did I put my instruction leaflet?"

She looked under the counter and on the shelves but she could not find it anywhere.

"Bother," she said. "I can't do my crochet without it."

"Good morning," said Miss Hubbard. "What are you looking for, Mrs Goggins?"

Mrs Goggins explained what had happened.

"Dear, oh dear," tutted Miss Hubbard. "How annoying. It didn't drop down the back of anything, did it?"

Miss Hubbard helped Mrs Goggins look around the Post Office again but they did not find the leaflet.

"I'll have to start again with another pattern," Mrs Goggins moaned. "And it was such a nice design."

At that moment, Pat's van drew up outside the Post Office.

"Hello again," he said as he came in. "Look what I found among the letters!" Pat held up the missing leaflet.

"Oh thank you, Pat!" cried Mrs Goggins. "I've been looking everywhere for it."

"I must have picked it up with the post by mistake," said Pat.

But Mrs Goggins was too busy to listen to him.

"Three trebles, miss one . . ." she was muttering as she began to crochet.

Jess makes a friend

1 One day, Jess was playing in the garden. He was hiding in the grass and chasing leaves. He was having good fun.

2 The wind blew the leaves up in a flurry. Jess dashed under the hedge. He peeped out to see where they were.

3 Then he noticed a pair of dark eyes watching him. He looked closer and saw a snout as well. Jess had a friend!

4 Jess sniffed at the little animal. But the little animal scurried under the hedge to hide. Jess squeezed in after it.

5 Jess tried to touch it. Suddenly, the eyes and snout disappeared. Now Jess could only see a spiky ball.

6 Jess sniffed and stretched out his paw again. The spiky ball did not move so Jess patted it gingerly with his paw.

7 Then he had a nasty surprise. The spikes were sharp and dug into his paw. Jess leapt back and ran to Pat.

8 "What's wrong, Jess?" said Pat when he saw Jess limping. "Have you hurt your paw?" Pat gently lifted him up.

9 "Nothing sticking into it," said Pat. "It will soon be better. Let's see what you hurt it on." They went into the garden.

10 By this time, the hedgehog had unrolled itself and was walking across the grass. "Aha!" said Pat.

11 "I know something hedgehogs and cats like," Pat said. He brought out a big saucer of milk for them both.

Can you help the hedgehog find its way through the leaves to Jess?

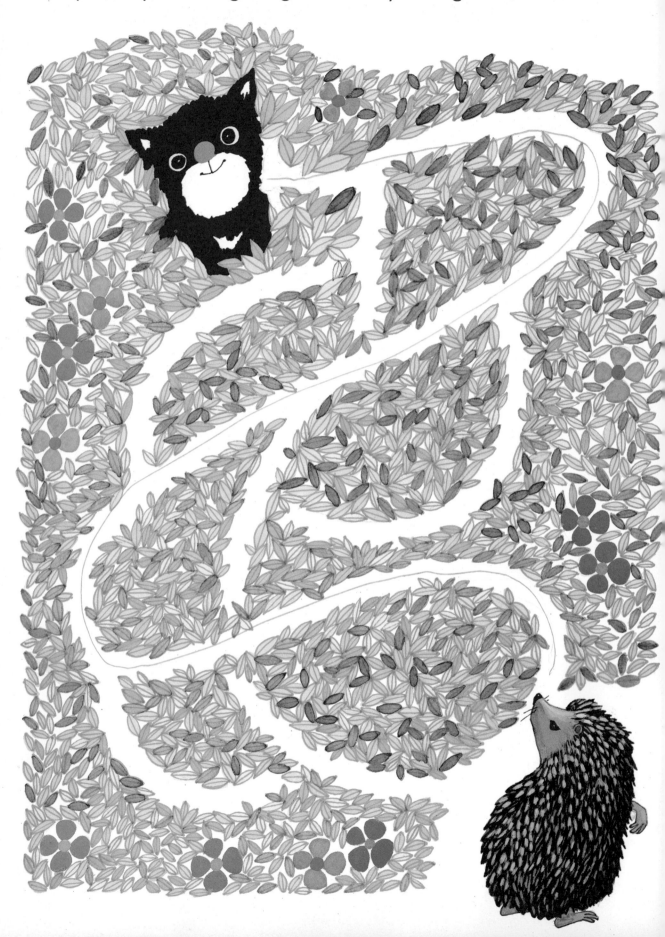

Wheat hedgehog

 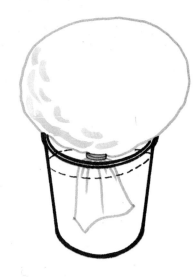

Place a handful of wheat in a square of muslin.

Make it into a ball and tie with a rubber band to leave a tail. Sit it in a glass of water so that the tail is wet. Draw eyes and a nose on the ball.

In a few days, your wheat hedgehog will start to grow!

You could give it a name.

Miss Hubbard bakes a cake

1 Miss Hubbard was baking a cake. "Rub in the butter," she re[ad] from the recipe book. "Add two eggs." She looked in the fridg[e.]

2 There were no eggs left. "Oh, dear," she said. "I'll have to go over to Thompson Ground for some."

3 Miss Hubbard pedalled along the ro[ad] and up a hill. It was hard work but downhill was easy. She whizzed alor[g.]

4 But then there was a hissing noise and the front tyre went slowly down. "Oh my hat!" she said. "A puncture!"

5 "And I've forgotten my repair kit. I'll have to walk." Then she saw Peter Fogg's tractor. "I'll borrow it," she said[.]

6 Miss Hubbard drove the tractor out of the field and up the road. "This is better," she said. "I'll soon be there."

7 Pat had to swerve to avoid her coming around a corner. "Goodness me," he said. "Miss Hubbard is in a hurry!"

8 Then he saw her bicycle lying at the roadside. "I'll drop it off at Ted's," said Pat. "He'll soon have it fixed for her."

9 Meanwhile, Miss Hubbard reached the farm. "Half a dozen eggs please," she said. Then she drove off again.

10 When she arrived home, Pat and Peter Fogg were waiting. "Thanks for the tractor, Peter," she said.

11 "Ted's fixing your bike," said Pat. "Oh, good," she said. "You can all have some cake when it's ready."

A picture to colour

Postman Pat's pineapple delight

Postman Pat loves cakes and puddings. Here is one of his favourite recipes.

Place trifle sponges in a bowl. Spread jam on top. Cover with crushed pineapple and whipped cream. Pop a cherry on top and it is ready to eat. It is even tastier if you can wait a few hours until all the juices have soaked into the sponge cakes!

1 "That old tree in the churchyard is not looking good," said the Reverend Timms. "It might topple over."

2 "I think it had better come down," said Ted. "Before it does any damage. I'll get Alf to come and help me."

3 Ted and Alf climbed up the big tree and lopped off the smaller branches with a chain-saw. "Bzzz," it went.

4 Pat drove past in his van. "It will look funny without that tree," he told Jess. Alf cut off another branch. "Bzzz."

Ted and Alf sawed through the bigger branches. "It's rotten inside," said Alf. "It could have fallen at any time."

6 They chopped down the big trunk. "Timber! Watch out!" shouted Ted as it fell. Now only the stump was left.

Alf used his tractor to pull out the old stump. The Reverend Timms brought out a young oak tree to plant.

8 When Pat drove past later, there was the new tree planted in the churchyard. "It will soon grow bigger," he said.

What can you find hidden amongst the leaves?

The Reverend Timms cannot read his book because he has lost his spectacles. Can you find them for him?

A quiet spot

The Reverend Timms was sitting in his study reading a book. It was a very interesting book and he was enjoying it. All was quiet, only the clock's tick disturbed the silence. Suddenly, the noise of the vacuum cleaner started up.

"Oh dear, oh dear," said the Reverend Timms. "I'd forgotten Mrs A. the cleaning lady came today."

The vacuum cleaner roared up and down the hall.

"I can't read with all that noise," muttered the Reverend Timms. "I'll go and sit outside in the sun."

He took a chair and sat down in the churchyard.

"TRATA TRATA TRATA TRAT.

"Goodness me, whatever is that?" exclaimed the Reverend Timms, jumping up to see what was going on.

Some roadworkers were digging up the street.

"Oh no," complained the Reverend. "I can't read with that racket. Where can I find a quiet spot?" He looked around and smiled. "The very place," he said.

The church was quiet as the Reverend Timms made his way up the aisle. He found a nice comfortable seat and began to read. Then the door opened and Miss Hubbard and Mrs Pottage came in. They were carrying bunches of flowers and Mrs Pottage had a duster. Their voices echoed around the church.

"Oh dear," the Reverend Timms said to himself. "They're going to tidy up and do the flowers. I'd better slip out and leave them to it."

The Reverend Timms took his book and walked along the road out of the village. Then he found just what he was looking for. He climbed a fence into a field and sat down under a tree.

"Peace at last," he said, as he settled down to read. "Nobody will disturb me here." He waved to Postman Pat who was driving along on the road below and opened his book.

The police dog trials

1 'POLICE DOG TRIALS' read the notice in the Post Office. "I must go to them," said Pat. "P.C. Selby is taking part."

2 At the trials, policemen ran around an obstacle course with their dogs. The dogs had to jump over fences.

3 P.C. Selby came out with his dog, Cora. "Ready?" he said. "Off we go." P.C. Selby started to run.

4 Cora followed him around the course. "She is doing well," Pat said to the twins who were there with Betsy.

5 Alf had Towser on a strong lead. "I don't want him to get free and ruin it all," said Alf. "He's a mischief maker."

6 "P.C. Selby's time is good," Colonel Forbes said. "He's in the lead." Snap sat beside him and barked.

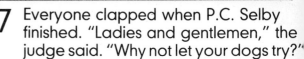

7 Everyone clapped when P.C. Selby finished. "Ladies and gentlemen," the judge said. "Why not let your dogs try?"

8 Katy and Tom ran on with Betsy. She could not jump the fences so she ran under them. "Good dog," they said.

9 Towser dashed off. "Come here!" shouted Alf. Towser ran into a tunnel just as Snap ran in the other end!

10 "Come out, Snap!" yelled Colonel Forbes. "Towser!" yelled Alf. The tunnel collapsed. "What next?" said Alf.

11 "They'll never be police dogs," said Colonel Forbes. "Never mind," said P.C. Selby. "They make good pets."

Katy and Tom's word game

Katy and Tom Pottage have written the word 'dog' ten times in this box of letters. Can you find them? Yes

m	d	c	e	d	w	b	c
a	o	m	r	o	s	v	d
z	g	d	o	g	e	f	h
x	p	o	c	z	v	d	c
d	o	g	m	s	x	o	e
o	n	e	a	d	o	g	d
g	d	o	g	o	m	s	r
p	c	o	s	g	f	h	n

Miss Hubbard is looking after her cousin Maude's Great Dane. What will she give him to eat?

The fancy dress parade

1 'FANCY DRESS PARADE TODAY' the notice in the Post Office read. "I'll go in for that," said Pat. "I wonder what I could wear?"

2 Pat drove to Greendale Farm. Mrs Pottage and the twins were busy. "What are you doing?" Pat said.

3 "It's our fancy dress costume," said Tom. "We're going as . . . " "Ssh!" said Katy. "It is a secret." "Oh!" said Pat.

4 At Thompson Ground, Bill was cutting up a cardboard box. "What are you going as?" Pat asked. Bill just smiled.

5 "Have you any ideas what to wear?" said Alf. "Not yet," Pat replied. "Have you?" "I might," said Alf, grinning.

6 When Pat arrived home, he looked for something to dress up in. "Here's a sheet," said Sara. "Go as an Arab."

7 Pat wrapped the sheet around him. Sara tied a tea-cloth on his head. "Will anyone recognise me?" he said.

8 Pat did not notice Sara taking away his uniform. "I'm ready now!" Pat called. "Let's go!" They drove to the hall.

9 Katy and Tom were already there. "What a clever idea," said Pat. Bill Thompson came as a television!

10 "And now the parade is about to begin," announced Bill. "But where's Alf?" Pat asked, looking around.

11 "Here I am," Alf said. Pat started to laugh. "Well I never!" he cried. "You look just like me." Everyone cheered.

Imagine if everyone dressed-up as Postman Pat!
Which postman is the real Pat?

You could dress-up like this. Make your costumes from card and crêpe paper. Bill Thompson's television is a box with plastic bottle-tops as knobs. The aerial is made from the lid of a jar, pipe-cleaners and ping-pong balls.

The missing eggs

1 Dorothy Thompson was looking cross when Pat arrived at Thompson Ground. "Hello there," he said. "Whatever is the matter?"

2 "It's those hens," said Dorothy. "I can't find where they are laying their eggs. I've looked everywhere for them."

3 "I'll help you," offered Pat. "I'll look in the cowshed." Pat peered in every nook and cranny but saw nothing.

4 Then he spotted one in the calves pen. "What a silly place to lay an egg," he said, reaching out to grab hold of it.

5 But one of the calves came to see what Pat was doing and stood on the egg. "Pity," said Pat. "It was big, too."

6 The hens watched Pat as he searched the hayshed. Jess helped him look. Soon Pat was covered in bits of straw.

7 "You look like a scarecrow!" said Dorothy. "Found any eggs yet?" "Only a squashed one," said Pat, laughing.

8 "Ssh! I just heard something," said Dorothy. Pat listened. "I can't hear anything at all," he whispered.

9 Pat listened again. "Yes I can," he said. "A sort of cheep cheep." "Let's see where it's coming from," said Dorothy.

10 They hunted through the straw. Then in a dark corner they found a hen. They could hear lots of cheeping.

11 Under her were chicks. "So that's where the eggs went!" Dorothy whispered. "The hen hatched them!"

Dorothy Thompson's hens

Two of these hens look
exactly the same.
Can you spot them?

POSTMAN PAT COMPETITION
4 Fabulous 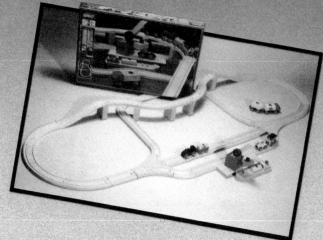 Wooden Railway Sets to be Won!

Brio's largest Railway Set 33143 comes complete with an Engine, 3 Wagons, 16 Curved 3 + 5 different sized Straight Tracks, 2 + 1 different sized Switching Tracks, 1 Crossing Track, 2 Ascending Tracks, 2 Supports, a Crane, Container Lorry with Wagon, a Container Boat and a Quay Berth, making a superb start to creating a 'Dockside' Railway.

Katy and Tom are singing nursery rhymes but they cannot remember all the words. Can you fill in the missing words from the first lines of the five nursery rhymes below? Write the five words on a postcard along with your age, name, address and parent's or guardian's signature and send it to: **Postman Pat Annual Competition**
4, Clareville Grove
LONDON
SW7 5AR

Closing date for the competition is January 30th 1987.
The first 4 correct entries drawn after the closing date will each be awarded a Brio Railway Set as described above.

RULES

1. Only entries written on a postcard or the back of an envelope will be accepted.

2. The competition is open to readers in the UK only.

3. Employees and their families of Argus Consumer Publications Ltd., Brio and their agents are not eligible to enter.

4. No correspondence will be entered into.

5. The Editor's decision is final.

THE COMPETITION

1. Oranges and *Lemons*, say the bells of St Clement's.

2. Hey diddle, diddle, the *cat* and the fiddle.

3. Hickory, dickory, dock. The *mouse* ran up the clock.

4. Sing a song of *sixpence*, a pocket full of rye.

5. Jack and Jill went up the hill to fetch a pail of *water*.

1 Pat was decorating Julian's bedroom. "Can you manage on your own?" asked Sara. "I'm going out." "Of course," said Pat.

2 "I'll paint the ceiling first," Pat said to Jess. Pat climbed up the ladder and began. "Pom te pom," he sang.

3 But the paint was runny and blobs fell on his head. "Bother," said Pat. Jess ran and hid. He did not like paint.

4 Pat put on an old hat. "That's better," he said. "It doesn't matter if the hat has paint on it." Soon he had finished.

5 "Now for the wallpaper," said Pat. He cut a length and pasted it. "It's very sticky," he said, trying to fold it up.

6 Pat climbed up the ladder. He did not notice he was standing on the paper. Rip! It tore in two. "Oh, no!" he cried.

7 Pat pasted some more paper. He climbed up again and stuck it on. "I'm sticking, too!" he said.

8 Jess watched Pat hang the wallpaper. At last the first piece was up. "I'll never finish it at this rate," groaned Pat.

9 Then there was a knock at the door. It was Ted. "You could do with a hand, Pat," he said, looking at the mess.

10 In no time at all, Ted had papered the bedroom. "Thanks, Ted," said Pat. "You've done a good job."

11 Sara was delighted. "Wasn't it hard?" she asked. "Oh, it was no bother at all," said Pat, winking at Jess.